This Warne book belongs to:

To *Achille* and *Aube*

First published 2015 by Walker Books Ltd, 87 Vauxhall Walk, London SE11 5HJ

This edition published 2016

2 4 6 8 10 9 7 5 3 1

© 2015 Petr Horáček

The right of Petr Horáček to be identified as author/illustrator of this work has been asserted
by him in accordance with the Copyright, Designs and Patents Act 1988

This book has been set in WBHoráček

Printed in China

British Library Cataloguing in Publication Data:
a catalogue record for this book is available from the British Library

ISBN 978-1-4063-6564-1

www.walker.co.uk

WALKER BOOKS
AND SUBSIDIARIES

LONDON • BOSTON • SYDNEY • AUCKLAND

Petr Horáček

# The Mouse
# Who Reached
# the Sky

One morning Little Mouse looked up at
the tree and saw something red and shiny
hanging from a branch.
"Oh, what a beautiful marble. I would
like to have it," she thought.

But as much
as she tried,

Little Mouse couldn't
reach it by herself.

"I need help," she said.
"I'll go and ask my
friend Mole.

We can play with the
marble together."

"Hello, Mole, are you there?"
called Little Mouse. "I've just seen
a beautiful marble hanging
from the tree!"

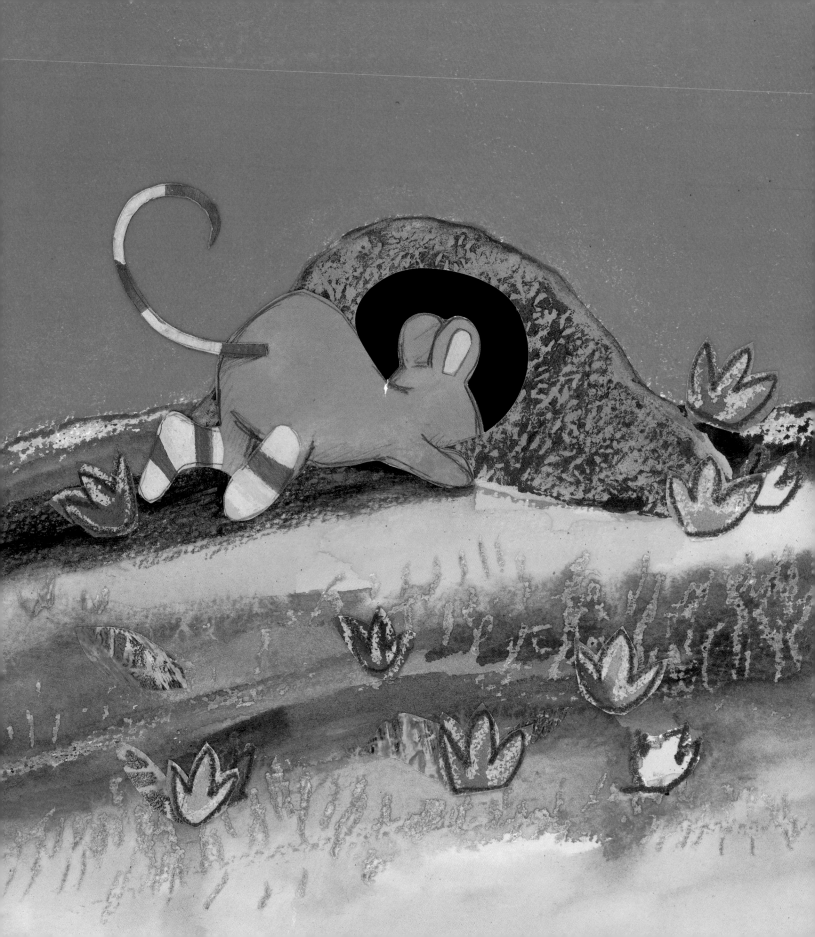

"It's red and shiny. If you help me reach
it, we can play with it together!"
"A marble? How exciting!
Of course I'll help," said Mole.

"Silly Mouse," said Mole. "That's not a marble. It's a red, shiny balloon.

We can use it to fly!" Mole stretched and jumped

as high as he could,
but he couldn't reach
it by himself.

"We need more help,"
said Mole.

"Hello, Rabbit," said Little Mouse.
"We've seen a beautiful red balloon in the tree.
If you help us reach it, we can use it to fly!"
"What a great idea," said Rabbit.
"Of course I'll help."

"Silly Mouse and Mole," laughed Rabbit. "That's not a balloon.

It's a big, shiny ball. We can play catch with it!" He stretched and jumped,

but he couldn't
reach it by himself,
either.

"We need someone
taller than me," said Rabbit.
"But no one is that tall!"

"Somebody taller than you?"
shouted Little Mouse.
"I KNOW!"

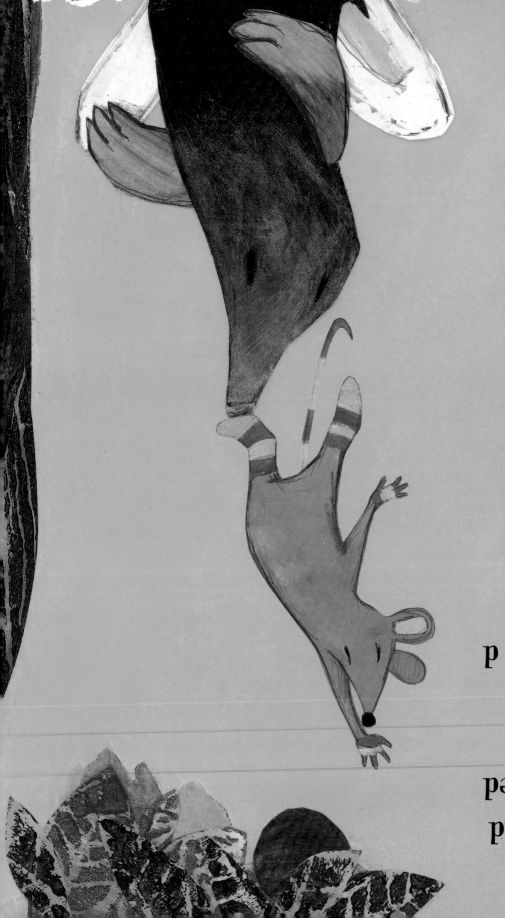

So Mole climbed
on top of Rabbit and
Little Mouse climbed
on top of Mole.
Together, they
stretched
and
stretched
and they
wobbled
and
wobbled
and
they
wobbled...

# CRASH!

They all fell down!
Little Mouse, Mole and Rabbit
hit the ground so hard that
the tree shook ...

and down came not one,
but hundreds of red, shiny
**things!**

"Look," said Rabbit, "we've all been silly. It wasn't a marble or a balloon. It wasn't a ball, either! It was a delicious cherry and now we have lots of them to eat."
"Just like magic," said Little Mouse. "Look what we three can do when we help each other!"
And they all laughed.

# Other books by Petr Horáček

 Silly Suzy Goose — Petr Horáček
978-1-4063-0458-9

 Look Out, Suzy Goose — Petr Horáček
978-1-4063-1764-0

 Suzy Goose and the Christmas Star — Petr Horáček
978-1-4063-2621-5

 ELEPHANT — Petr Horáček
978-1-4063-2441-9

 The Fly — Petr Horáček
978-1-4063-3073-1

 Puffin Peter — Petr Horáček
978-1-4063-3776-1

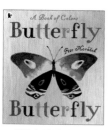 A Book of Colors: Butterfly Butterfly — Petr Horáček
978-1-4063-4006-8

 A Peep-through Counting Book: When the Moon Smiled — Petr Horáček
978-0-7445-7047-2

 BLUE PENGUIN — Petr Horáček
978-1-4063-5828-5

## Also featuring Little Mouse

 A Peep-through Story Book: A New House for Mouse — Petr Horáček
978-1-4063-0122-9

 A Peep-through Story Book: The Mouse Who Ate the Moon — Petr Horáček
978-1-4063-6067-7

 Beep Beep — Petr Horáček
978-1-4063-2505-8

 Choo Choo — Petr Horáček
978-1-4063-2506-5

 Flutter by, butterfly — Petr Horáček
978-1-4063-2507-2

 Hello, little bird — Petr Horáček
978-1-4063-2508-9

 Run, mouse, run! — Petr Horáček
978-1-4063-2509-6

 Strawberries are red — Petr Horáček
978-1-4063-2510-2

 This little cat — Petr Horáček
978-1-4063-2511-9

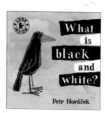 What is black and white? — Petr Horáček
978-1-4063-2512-6

 turn the wheel: Night Night — Petr Horáček
978-1-4063-2966-7

 turn the wheel: Creepy Crawly — Petr Horáček
978-1-4063-2967-4

 flip-flap fun: Honk Honk! Baa Baa! — Petr Horáček
978-1-4063-4375-5

 flip-flap fun: Time For Bed — Petr Horáček
978-1-4063-4376-2

 turn the wheel: A Surprise For Tiny Mouse — Petr Horáček
978-1-4063-5545-1

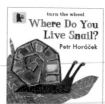 turn the wheel: Where Do You Live Snail? — Petr Horáček
978-1-4063-5546-8

Available from all good booksellers

www.walker.co.uk